Meet Dizzy Dinosaur!

by Jack Tickle

tiger tales

Hello, everyone.
Meet Dizzy Dinosaur!

Over here,
Dizzy!
We're
behind
YOU!

Isn't he cute? Dizzy loves to be tickled. Come on, everyone—let's tickle Dizzy on his tummy!

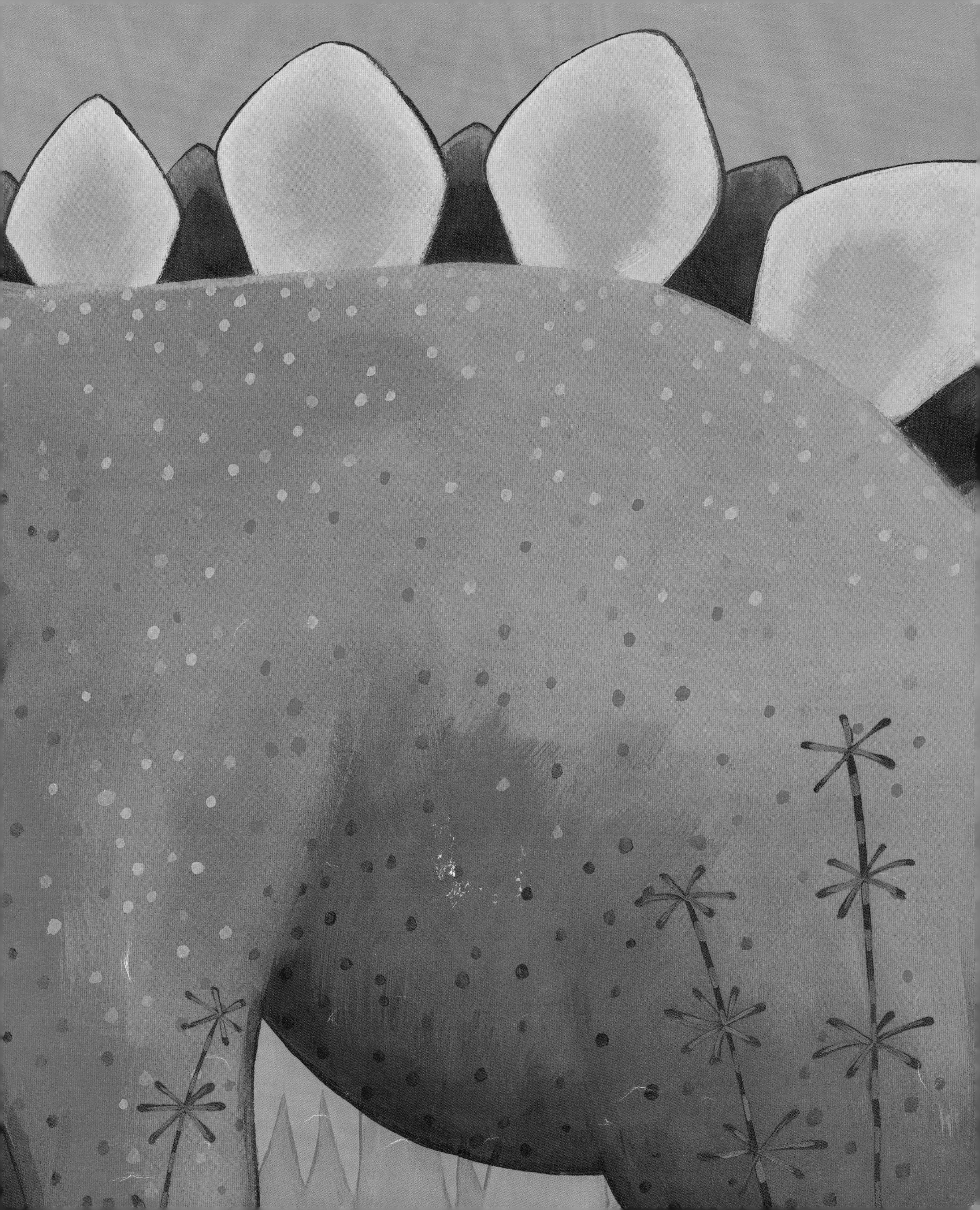

Hee hee hee!

Oops!

We've tickled Dizzy
a bit too much.

Look out,
Dizzy!

Splash!

Poor soggy Dizzy!
Let's shake the book
up and down.
That will dry him off.

Whoa!

That’s a bit too shaky!

Hic!

Hic!

Hic!

Uh-oh!

Now Dizzy has the hiccups!
How can we stop them?
I know! We can surprise him.
Let's all shout "Boo!"
on three:
one . . .
two . . .
three . . .

Boo!

Ooooh!

Oh, no, Dizzy! We're sorry we scared you!

We have to help Dizzy down from the tree. Let's turn the book sideways.

Oops!
Poor Dizzy has
bumped his bottom.
Come
here,
Dizzy!

We can cheer you up!

Coming!

Slow down, Dizzy!
You're going too fast!

Crash!

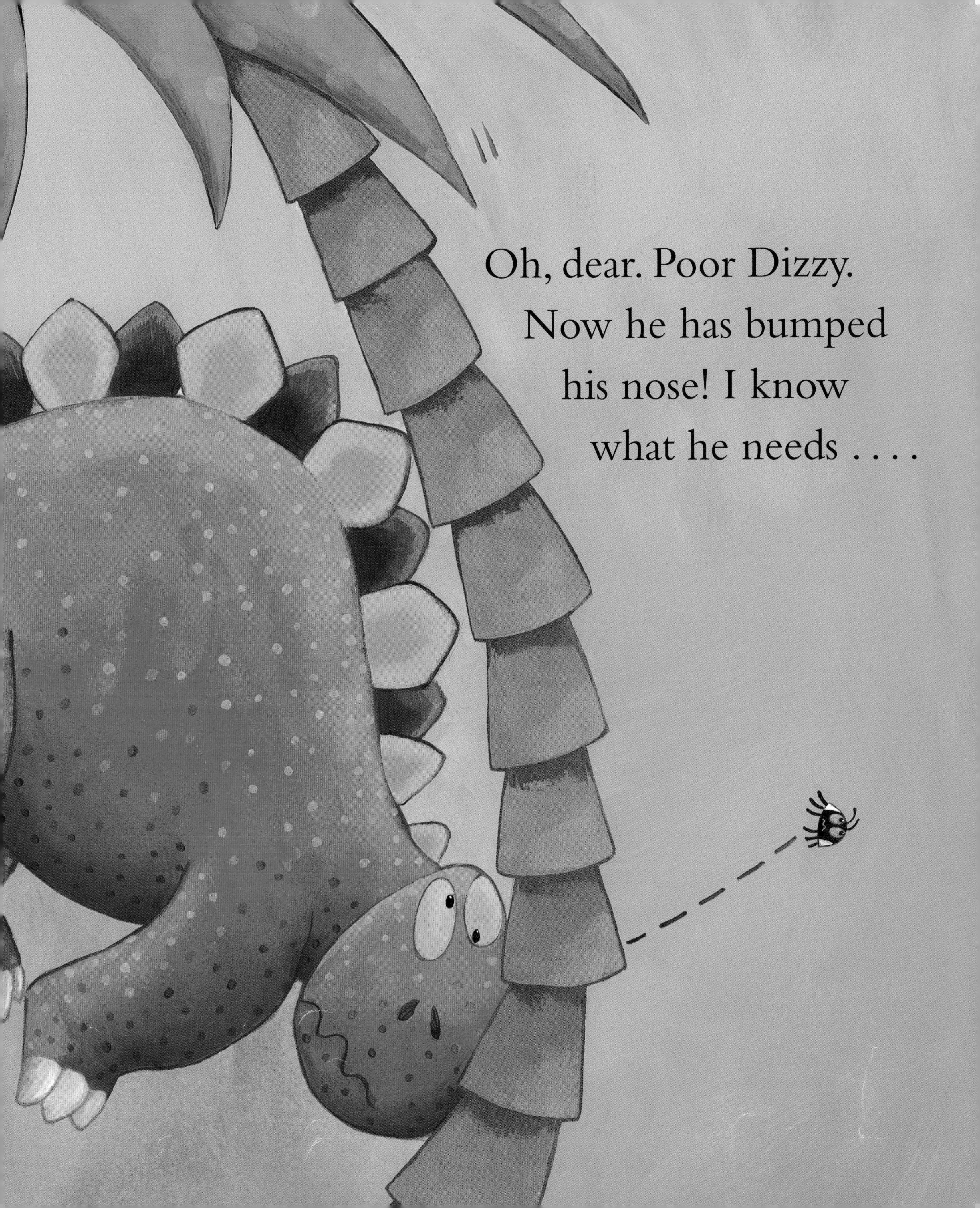

Oh, dear. Poor Dizzy.
Now he has bumped
his nose! I know
what he needs . . . .

Let's all give Dizzy
a great big kiss.
That's better.
Bye-bye,
Dizzy.
See you
soon!

Awww!